spot

MIGHTY MACHINES

DUMP TRUCKS

by Mari Schuh

AMICUS | AMICUS INK

bed

ram

Look for these words and pictures as you read.

tailgate

cab

Here comes a dump truck!
What can it do?

A dump truck
carries heavy loads.
Then it dumps the loads.
Look at it dump the rocks!

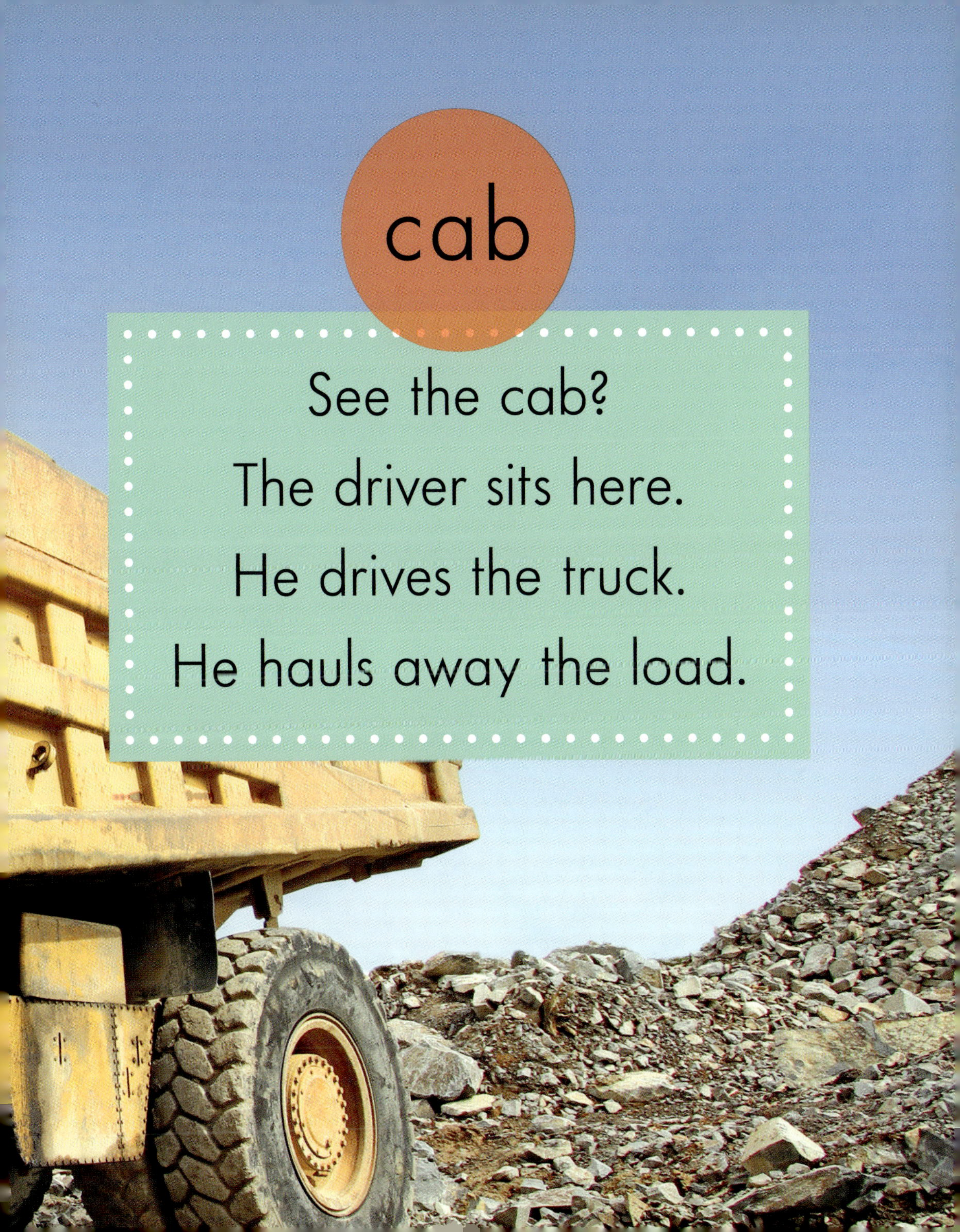

cab

See the cab?
The driver sits here.
He drives the truck.
He hauls away the load.

bed

See the bed?
It holds the load.
It can tilt.

See the ram?
It lifts the bed high.
Oil helps the ram move.

ram

See the tailgate? It opens.
Now the load pours out.

tailgate

A dump truck moves snow.
See it go!

bed

ram

Did you find?

tailgate

cab

Spot is published by Amicus and Amicus Ink
P.O. Box 1329, Mankato, MN 56002
www.amicuspublishing.us

Library of Congress Cataloging-in-Publication Data:
Names: Schuh, Mari C., 1975- author.
Title: Dump trucks / by Mari Schuh.
Description: Mankato, Minnesota : Amicus, 2018. | Series: Spot. Mighty machines | Audience: K to grade 3.
Identifiers: LCCN 2016048894 (print) | LCCN 2016050100 (ebook) | ISBN 9781681511023 (library binding) | ISBN 9781681522135 (pbk.) | ISBN 9781681511924 (e-book)
Subjects: LCSH: Dump trucks--Juvenile literature.
Classification: LCC TL230.15 .S42 2018 (print) | LCC TL230.15 (ebook) | DDC 629.224--dc23
LC record available at https://lccn.loc.gov/2016048894

Printed in the United States of America

HC 10 9 8 7 6 5 4 3 2 1
PB 10 9 8 7 6 5 4 3 2 1

To Jadyn —MS

Wendy Dieker, editor
Deb Miner, series designer
Aubrey Harper, book designer
Holly Young, photo researcher

Photos by Alamy 12–13; Dreamstime cover, 4–5, 10–11; iStock 1, 6–7, 8–9, 14–15; Shutterstock 3